Mrs. Church's Garden

Mrs. Church's Garden

ej Ndeto

Illustrated by Zascha Harder

ELM HILL

A Division of
HarperCollins Christian Publishing

www.elmhillbooks.com

Mrs. Church's Garden

Published in Nashville, Tennessee, by Elm Hill, an imprint of Thomas Nelson. Elm Hill and Thomas Nelson are registered trademarks of HarperCollins Christian Publishing, Inc.

Elm Hill titles may be purchased in bulk for educational, business, fund-raising, or sales promotional use. For information, please e-mail SpecialMarkets@ThomasNelson.com.

Publisher's Note: This novel is a work of fiction. Names, characters, places, and incidents are either products of the author's imagination or used fictitiously. All characters are fictional, and any similarity to people living or dead is purely coincidental.

Library of Congress Cataloging-in-Publication Data

Library of Congress Control Number: 2019909187

ISBN 978-1-400325900 (Paperback)
ISBN 978-1-400325917 (eBook)

Mrs. Church's garden was a jungle.

Everywhere you looked, there was something growing.
Every time of the year, there was something blooming.

There were roses and iris and orchids. An orange tree stood in the corner; its branches lush with fruit.

A plum tree stood by the gate and a cherry tree stood guard near the front door.

In the middle, sat a pond filled with lily pads, goldfish, water snails, and one giant bullfrog named Sparky.

When it rained, the drops sparkled like diamonds across the leaves.

When the sun shone, the garden was alive with feathers and wings.

Yes, Mrs. Church's garden was a jungle.

But it was her jungle and she took great care of it—weeding and raking, planting and trimming, and loving every square inch.

People in the neighborhood took the time to stop and stare in wonder at the magic of Mrs. Church's garden.

They would smell the flowers that bloomed near the sidewalk. They would watch the birds as they danced through the air. They would smile at Sparky the Frog sunning himself on a rock.

It was Mrs. Church's garden. It was a jungle and the neighbors loved it.

JR lived down the street from Mrs. Church's garden. She was happy to have reached an age when her mother would let her walk home from school by herself.

Carefully, she would walk to the crosswalk, push the button, and wait.

When the lights changed, JR would quickly rush to the other side and wander slowly down the sidewalk,

stopping for a chat with the ants that are making their way home.

Mrs. Shelby, who lived in the
blue house with the red door,
would wave as she went by
and ask about her day.

Mr. Hawkins, who liked to sit on his porch
and watch the birds, would point out a new
bird's nest.

Mrs. Church would let JR
stop and pick a few flowers
for her mother.

Then, one day, Mrs. Church broke her hip.

And while her bones healed, the garden didn't wait.

Weeds grew. Flowers died.

Little bushes became big bushes.

Big bushes became monsters with thorns.

Sticky vines that would sneak out and grab onto a wary passerby.

But Mrs. Church could not move to care for her garden.

Neighbors would hurry by quickly.

They would not look at the dying flower petals that had fallen on the sidewalk.

They could not watch the birds for the bushes were too thick.

They could not see Sparky the Frog sunning himself on a rock.

It was a jungle and the neighbors no longer enjoyed it.

JR started to worry about the vines that tickled her as she wandered past.

She dreaded the walk home, dragging her feet past Mrs. Shelby's house, slowing to a crawl at Mr. Hawkins'.

Then, gathering herself up, JR would make a mad dash past Mrs. Church's garden.

But the plants would reach out, grab her, and hold her tight.

Mrs. Shelby and Mr. Hawkins watched her progress daily as she made her way between the branches and the vines of Mrs. Church's garden.

They watched as she'd gear herself up for the run between the leaves and thorns.

They watched as the vines would tangle her up and try and hold her close.

Then, one day, JR just stopped and did not move.

Mrs. Shelby and Mr. Hawkins watched as JR slowly pulled off her backpack, put it on the sidewalk, and opened it up.

They watched as JR pulled a pair of garden shears out and gently took hold of the vine closest to her ...

Snip.

And it was on the ground.

JR took a step forward and took hold of another vine.

Snip.

She grabbed another then another and another and another and, soon, a pile of vines surrounded JR and Mrs. Church's jungle began to look like a garden again.

And, as JR made her way around Mrs. Church's garden, Mrs. Shelby and Mr. Hawkins pulled themselves up off their chairs and made their way over and began to clear the pieces away.

Neighbors stopped to help and, soon, all was right again. Mrs. Church's garden was a jungle and it was lovely.

People in the neighborhood took the time to stop and stare in wonder at the magic of her garden.

They would smell the flowers that bloomed near the sidewalk.
They would watch the birds as they danced through the air.
They would smile at Sparky the Frog sunning himself on a rock.
It was Mrs. Church's garden. It was a jungle and the neighbors loved it.

When Mrs. Church came home from the hospital, her garden was lovely.

As she slowly made her way up her front walk, she smiled at her flowers.

She took a moment to touch the leaves on her roses, to smell the orange blossoms.

She took a seat on the bench at the pond, watched Sparky sit in the sun, and smiled at her beautiful garden.

She was sitting there when JR came home from school.

JR didn't see Mrs. Church sitting in the sun as she put down her backpack and pulled out her garden shears. She didn't see Mrs. Church as she clipped a dead rose head, as she pulled a few weeds, as she snipped a wayward vine.

But, when she saw Mrs. Church, she smiled.

And Mrs. Church smiled.

And Mrs. Church opened her arms to JR as she moved in for a hug.

They sat there, together, in her beautiful garden.

And everywhere you looked, there was something growing. Every time of the year, there was something blooming.

Mrs. Church's garden was a jungle and it was lovely.

CPSIA information can be obtained
at www.ICGtesting.com
Printed in the USA
LVHW050401270919
632431LV00003B/10/P